THE
GRAND
CANYON

JENNY MARKERT

THE CHILD'S WORLD

Designed and Photographed by:
MICHAEL GEORGE

Distributed to schools and libraries in the United States by
ENCYCLOPAEDIA BRITANNICA EDUCATIONAL CORP.
310 South Michigan Avenue
Chicago, Illinois 60604

Library of Congress Cataloging-in-Publication Data
Markert, Jenny.
The Grand Canyon / by Jenny Markert.
p. cm.
Summary: The author describes what she saw on a
backpacking trip in the Grand Canyon.
ISBN 0-89565-856-9
1. Grand Canyon (Ariz.)--Description and travel--Juvenile
literature. 2. Backpacking--Arizona--Grand Canyon--
Juvenile literature. 3. Grand Canyon National Park (Ariz.)--
Juvenile literature. [1. Grand Canyon National Park (Ariz.)
2. National parks and reserves. 3. Backpacking.] I. Title.
F788.M37 1992   91-41152
917.91' 320453--dc20   CIP
                                                           AC

I was eight years old the first time I heard about the Grand Canyon. My best friend had spent the summer in Arizona and told me of the spectacle. He said the canyon was bigger than the deepest ravine we had ever explored. Since we were the neighborhood's most accomplished explorers, I had my doubts. Ever since, I dreamed of seeing the Grand Canyon myself.

I finally had my chance during the summer of my twenty-sixth year. After driving across half the United States, my traveling companion Mike and I reached the northwest corner of Arizona. Following a torn and tattered atlas, we drove on a narrow dirt road surrounded by birches, aspens, and lofty pines. Gradually, thorny bushes and cacti replaced the shady trees. The sun grew brighter and the air hotter. Then, suddenly, the earth dropped out in front of the car. I had finally reached the edge of the Grand Canyon.

Mike and I were born and raised on the flat grasslands of Minnesota. The size of the canyon in front of us was foreign and intimidating. We cautiously opened the car doors and inched our way to the edge. The wind blew so hard that nearby bushes and trees danced and swayed. It made me dizzy to stand so near such a deep chasm. Even with my eyes closed, I felt the empty, earthless hole beside me.

Far below, at the deepest part of the canyon, we saw the snakelike path of the Colorado River. As we stood a mile above its banks, the river looked like a peaceful

stream. Actually, it gushes with force and danger. In fact, the river is responsible for the gaping canyon itself.

Year by year and layer by layer, the Colorado River has eaten into the earth. It has been a very slow process. Scientists think that it began about 6 million years ago. Over this enormous span of time, the river has carried all the rock and dirt that used to fill the canyon downstream, hundreds of miles to the Gulf of California.

As I peered at the rocky walls, I imagined how other people felt when they first set eyes on the Grand Canyon. People first entered the canyon about 4,000 years ago. The drawings and buildings of these early Americans can still be found within the canyon. Miners, scientists, and adventurers began to explore the region about

200 years ago. Then, in the late 1800s, tourists began hiking into the canyon. Millions of people now visit the Grand Canyon every year.

After soaking in the sights, Mike and I started to plan our own adventure into the canyon. We decided to follow the Kiabab Trail, the canyon's main thoroughfare. From the canyon's North Rim, the trail plunges fourteen miles to the canyon floor, crosses the Colorado River, then climbs six miles to the South Rim. It takes about four days to travel the entire length of the trail. Unfortunately, we could get a campsite for only one night. On the main paths, the Grand Canyon is more like a backwoods city than an untamed wilderness. All the campsites along the Kiabab Trail were reserved for the rest of the summer.

A bit disappointed, we began our adventure early the next morning. From the moment we left the parking lot, every step we took was down, down, down, sinking us deeper and deeper into the earth. Our enthusiasm was quickly spent trying to keep our bodies from bouncing out of control. Within minutes, we were looking up at the canyon walls. In places, we had to strain our necks to see the top.

The pine trees and breezes of the high plateau quickly gave way to the shriveled cacti and heat of the inner canyon. The plateau has a climate similar to the northern United States. It is home to deer, squirrels, and singing birds. In the inner canyon, 100-degree temperatures and a severe lack of water make life scarce. Snakes, lizards, and buzzing insects are the only animals equipped to survive the harsh desert climate.

Like other highly traveled trails, the Kiabab Trail is made up of loose rocks, pebbles, and dirt. We were soon covered head to toe with fine, sootlike dust. To make matters worse, we often met mule packs carrying tourists up the trail. Not wanting to be trampled, we would edge off the side of the trail. There we would wait, surrounded by the dust, flies, and odors that follow a train of mules.

After one particularly dusty convoy of mules, we rounded a corner and were greeted by the sound of thunder. Water gushed from the canyon wall across the gully. Far below, the water collected in a stream and wound its way downhill. A variety of thirsty plants and animals clung

to life beside the stream. Bright green trees, shrubs, and grasses crowded the shore while birds and insects fluttered through the air.

We followed the stream downhill for the next two hours. By the time we reached our campsite, we had traveled seven miles. Our campsite, however, was far from remote. We were out in the open, with no trees for privacy or shade. Other campers were close; we could see and hear them easily. The campground's picnic tables and water faucets seemed out of place so far from civilization.

The local lizards didn't seem to mind the accommodations. They scampered around our feet, under the picnic table, and through the bushes. Two of them played tag by our campsite. Their tiny rib cages would pulsate whenever they stopped to catch their breath. Other lizards, less athletic than these, pressed their bodies into the ground to soak up the sun's warmth.

After dinner and a short rest, we left our campsite to explore the natural surroundings. Dense, prickly bushes made walking difficult near the creek, but the vegetation became sparse away from the water. Loose rocks and boulders littered the adjacent hillsides.

Although the Colorado River began carving the canyon about 6 million years ago, the rocks we walked on were much, much older. Those near the canyon rim are the youngest. They formed about 100 million years ago, when dinosaurs ruled the earth. The rocks we stumbled over formed 500 or 600 million years ago. Deeper in the

For the rest of the hike, we regretted that we didn't enjoy just one more glass of lemonade. The only thing that wet our lips was the warm water that we carried in our packs. We climbed uphill most of the time. Each steep climb ended in a sharp turn that tied it to the next steep climb. Back and forth we went, huffing and puffing and stopping often to catch our breath. Once again, the mule trains were a frequent nuisance.

We stopped for lunch—dried fruit and trail mix—two miles from the end of our uphill journey. After a rest that seemed far too brief, Mike and I nudged ourselves back on the trail. Despite the rest, our packs seemed heavier, our legs weaker, and the sun hotter. Each switchback seemed to be the last, but never was.

When we had given up on reaching the top altogether, suddenly we were there. I looked up and saw the sign that marked the end of the trail. At last, we dragged ourselves and our packs to the top of the canyon. I longed to leap into the air, but my weary legs would not permit such a display.

Back at the car, with our backpacks slumped at our feet, we stretched our stiff, tired legs. With a strange mixture of reluctance and enthusiasm, I stood up and wobbled to the canyon's edge. The steep, rocky walls stretched off into the distant haze. Looking into the canyon, I imagined a time before hikers, park rangers, and mule trains. I wondered how ancient people traveled in the canyon. How did they survive the heat? What did they eat and drink?

canyon, the rocks are older yet. Scientists estimate that some rocks near the banks of the Colorado River are 2 billion years old!

There are many rocks in the canyon that provide dramatic evidence of their age. They contain fossils—the remains of organisms that lived at the time of the rock's formation. Some fossils are recognizable—a dragonfly's wing, a leaf from a tree, or a reptile's footprint. Other fossils, like tribolites or brachiopods, do not look at all like animals we are familiar with. These tiny, prehistoric organisms were among the first living things on earth.

Our explorations were cut short when the sun sank below the canyon's rim. It was dark before we could stumble back to our campsite. We dozed off to sleep as the moon floated above the horizon.

What seemed like minutes later, I woke to fussing birds and fluttering butterflies. I lingered in my sleeping bag, watching hungry beetles look for breakfast on the ground beside me. As the sky turned blue, I heaved myself out of my nest. Soon, we were back on the trail, this time traveling up.

The first leg of our return journey was tolerable, even pleasant. The air was cool and the wind felt like feathers on my face. Just before the trail turned steeply upward, we passed a private home. The owner had created a wayside rest beside the desolate canyon highway. Beneath some shady trees, folding chairs and ice-cold lemonade enticed weary travelers. Spare change lay at the bottom of a dented tin can—gratuity for the cold drinks and shade.

The rocks around me felt so old. If the canyon walls were alive and could speak, imagine the tales they could tell. Stories of ancient organisms and primitive cultures, raging floods and ravaging winds. Imagine the sunsets, the moonlit nights, and the star-filled skies. Though it was a grueling adventure, the pain had already faded. After nearly twenty years of dreaming, I had finally explored the grandest canyon on earth.